LITTLE MISS
TINY
just the right size

Original concept by Roger Hargreaves
Illustrated and written by Adam Hargreaves

MR. MEN   LITTLE MISS

Little Miss Tiny lives in a mousehole in the dining-room of Home Farm.

One day she woke up early and decided to go exploring.

Exploring upstairs!

In all the time she had lived at Home Farm she had never been upstairs.

Well, when you are as small as Little Miss Tiny, a staircase is like a mountain.

Little Miss Tiny started to climb the stairs.

She climbed, and she climbed, and she climbed some more.

All the way to the top.

It took her nearly the whole morning!

Everything was very quiet because everyone had gone out for the day.

She wandered through the bedrooms.

She explored the bathroom.

And then she discovered the nursery.

Lying on the floor was a box with a hook on the lid.

She lifted the hook ...

... and got the fright of her life.

"Help!" she shrieked, and hid under the bed.

After a while she plucked up courage and peeked out.

"You silly-billy," she said to herself, "it's only a jack-in-the-box."

She began to look around.

It was wonderful.

She said, "How do you do," to a very serious-looking soldier.

She tickled a teddy bear.

And climbed a tower of blocks.

It was from the top of the blocks that Little Miss Tiny saw the most wonderful sight she had seen in all her tiny life.

A doll's house!

Little Miss Tiny opened the front door and went in.

Everything was just the right size for her.
The chairs, the table, the cups and even the stairs.

She went upstairs.

And lay down on the bed and closed her eyes.

She suddenly woke up with a start.

There, looking through the bedroom window of the doll's house, was the farm cat!

Little Miss Tiny didn't know what to do. How was she going to get back to her mousehole?

She went downstairs and through a door.

The farm cat watched her through the windows.

She found herself in a garage on the side of the doll's house, and in the garage was a wind-up toy car.

The little car gave her an idea.

She turned the key on the car, wound it up and jumped in.

The little car took off like a rocket through the little garage doors and straight through the cat's legs!

The car and Little Miss Tiny raced across the carpet, out through the door and down the landing.

Little Miss Tiny laughed with glee.

And then realised she had laughed too soon.

The car shot over the top step of the stairs and out into space and down ...

and down ...

and down ...

Little Miss Tiny shrieked.

With a SPLASH! she landed in the cat's bowl of milk at the bottom of the stairs.

She rushed through the hall, ran across the dining-room floor and back to the safety of her mousehole.

"Phew! That was close!" she said, with a big sigh of relief.

Well, a big sigh of relief for someone as tiny as Little Miss Tiny.

3 Sixteen Beautiful Fridge Magnets – any 2 for £2.00! inc.P&P

They're very special collector's items!
Simply tick your first and second* choices from the list below
of any 2 characters!

1st Choice

☐ Mr. Happy
☐ Mr. Lazy
☐ Mr. Topsy-Turvy
☐ Mr. Bounce
☐ Mr. Bump
☐ Mr. Small
☐ Mr. Snow
☐ Mr. Wrong

☐ Mr. Daydream
☐ Mr. Tickle
☐ Mr. Greedy
☐ Mr. Funny
☐ Little Miss Giggles
☐ Little Miss Splendid
☐ Little Miss Naughty
☐ Little Miss Sunshine

2nd Choice

☐ Mr. Happy
☐ Mr. Lazy
☐ Mr. Topsy-Turvy
☐ Mr. Bounce
☐ Mr. Bump
☐ Mr. Small
☐ Mr. Snow
☐ Mr. Wrong

☐ Mr. Daydream
☐ Mr. Tickle
☐ Mr. Greedy
☐ Mr. Funny
☐ Little Miss Giggles
☐ Little Miss Splendid
☐ Little Miss Naughty
☐ Little Miss Sunshine

*Only in case your first choice is out of stock.

CUT ALONG DOTTED LINE AND RETURN THIS WHOLE PAGE

--- TO BE COMPLETED BY AN ADULT ---

**To apply for any of these great offers, ask an adult to complete the coupon below and send it with
the appropriate payment and tokens, if needed, to MR. MEN OFFERS, PO BOX 7, MANCHESTER M19 2HD**

☐ Please send ____ Mr. Men Library case(s) and/or ____ Little Miss Library case(s) at £5.99 each inc P&P
☐ Please send a poster and door hanger as selected overleaf. I enclose six tokens plus a 50p coin for P&P
☐ Please send me ____ pair(s) of Mr. Men/Little Miss fridge magnets, as selected above at £2.00 inc P&P

Fan's Name _____

Address _____

_____ **Postcode** _____

Date of Birth _____

Name of Parent/Guardian _____

Total amount enclosed £ _____

☐ **I enclose a cheque/postal order payable to Egmont Books Limited**

☐ **Please charge my MasterCard/Visa/Amex/Switch or Delta account** (delete as appropriate)

Card Number

Expiry date ___ / ___   **Signature** _____

Please allow 28 days for delivery. We reserve the right to change the terms of this offer at any time
but we offer a 14 day money back guarantee. This does not affect your statutory rights.

MR.MEN   LITTLE MISS
Mr. Men and Little Miss™ & ©Mrs. Roger Hargreaves